MY FIRST
I Can Read Book®

Whose Hat Is It?

by Valeri Gorbachev

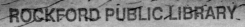

HarperCollins*Publishers*

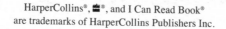

HarperCollins®, ♣®, and I Can Read Book®
are trademarks of HarperCollins Publishers Inc.

Whose Hat Is It?
Copyright © 2004 by Valeri Gorbachev
Printed in the U.S.A. All rights reserved.
www.harperchildrens.com

Library of Congress Cataloging-in-Publication Data
Gorbachev, Valeri.
Whose hat is it? / by Valeri Gorbachev.—1st ed.
p.   cm.—(My first I can read book)
Summary: When someone's hat blows off in the wind, Turtle
asks various animals if it belongs to one of them.
ISBN 0-06-053434-6 — ISBN 0-06-053435-4 (lib. bdg.)
[1. Hats—Fiction. 2. Turtles—Fiction. 3. Animals—Fiction.]
I. Title. II. Series.
PZ7.G6475Wk 2004
[E]—dc21
2003000505

1 2 3 4 5 6 7 8 9 10
❖
First Edition

To JoLyn Taylor-Brown
and Kent L. Brown

"Wow! Someone's hat
was blown off by the wind!"
Turtle said.

"Whose hat is it?"

"Is it your hat, Mouse?"

"It is not mine," Mouse said.

"Is it your hat, Rabbit?"

"It is not mine," Rabbit said.

"Is it your hat, Beaver?"

"It is not mine," Beaver said.

"Is it your hat, Crocodile?"

"It is not mine,"
Crocodile said.

"Whose hat is it?"

"It is mine," Elephant said.

"My hat was blown off
by the wind!"

"Thank you for finding it, Turtle!"

"You are welcome!"